The Little Mountain Goat

Written by XUE TAO

Ilustrated by WANG XIAOXIAO

Prunus Press USA

Original Title: 《小山羊走过田野》

The Little Mountain Goat

Written by Xue Tao

Illustrated by Wang Xiaoxiao

Translated by Scott Rainen

Designed by Brandy Ding

First edition 2022

ISBN: 978-1-61612-149-5

Prunus Press USA

A Note to English Readers

I was delighted to learn that an English translation of *The Little Mountain Goat* would be published—delighted to the point I couldn't sleep. In fact, it's in a sleepless state that I've decided to discuss the history of this book with you.

I've never written a book that fell into my lap from above, and this story is no exception.

My life has been just like that of the little mountain goat. I lived in a field in the northern part of Tieling, and I grew up too slowly. Slower than a tree. As a result, I spent most of my time tussling with my neighbor, Xiao Caizi. I was no match for him. At least, that was true until one day when my dad returned with a little mountain goat, a goat that could help me make up for lost ground. I led the goat over to Xiao Caizi, and it bleated wildly at him before charging. Caizi scurried away, and I knew I finally had the upper hand.

Xiao Caizi bitterly hated the mountain goat. He often hid behind the bushes, staring at the goat, and he came up with several mean nicknames as well—nicknames like "Dung-Goat." I wasn't a polite child, so I gave Xiao Caizi an even ruder nickname: "Snively." This was an appropriate form of retaliation.

One day, my dad sold the little mountain goat, so the creature disappeared from the field.

I ran into Xiao Caizi three days later, and I told him that I missed the little mountain goat. Much to my surprise, he replied that he also missed the goat.

And so it turned out that my arch-enemy also missed that same little goat. At that moment, I felt a closeness with Xiao Caizi.

The next day I went to Xiao Caizi and told him that I wanted to go to a field in the northern part of our village and find the mountain goat. I asked if he wanted to come along.

"I'll go with you," he replied.

So the two of us went off to find our "common" friend, the mountain goat. In this way, the two of us made peace. It was that simple.

Earlier this year, I wrote a story about a little mountain goat. I invoked the rights of an author—imagination, fiction—to produce a new experience.

I used Mandarin to write this story, and now you read it in English. Thanks to this little mountain goat, and an excellent translation, the two of us can traverse a linguistic barrier and become friends.

A single book is thus able to bring together such different perspectives and spirits. As an author, I can only feel exceptionally fortunate.

June 30, 2021
Written in a little wooden house.

The Little Mountain Goat

We'll be

in the same world

no matter

where we go.

ABOUT THE AUTHORS

Xue Tao, has been published more than 50 titles of Children's and YA , including *Bubble's Traveling, The Small Castle, Across the River, Shali and Stardust,* etc. His works won a number of prizes including Chinese Best Publications (books) Award, Taiwan Jiuge Modern Children's Literature Prize, Excellent Children's Literature Publishing Engineering Award etc., and have been translated into English, Japanese, Korean, Germany, Russian, Arabic, Farsi, Spanish, etc.

Wang Xiaoxiao, an independent illustrator, was major in Animation Design, has won the international awards many times, such as the Hiii Illustration award, Golden Pinwheel International Young Illustrator Competition Silver Award, Laureate Award for Chinese Children Books, and her work has been selected by the Bologna Illustration Exhibition, 2022.

Contents

The Little Mountain Goat

I encountered the little goat in a bog as she was eagerly licking ice at the frozen banks.

"Where did you come from?" I asked.

"I came down from the mountains to find something to eat, but the plants have been locked below a layer of ice."

"I feel like I've seen you. Long, long ago in a field somewhere."

"I think I've seen you too," she replied. "And you know what, you look like another goat. He lived in the same field as I did until one day he disappeared. It's said he went to a faraway place."

"I can take you to that old place. We can rediscover anything from the past."

"You're not lying?"

"I'm telling the truth. Let me say it again: it's the truth. I can say it 1,000 times if you like."

"People only tell lies 1,000 times. As for the truth, you only need to say it once."

"Then let's set off," I proclaimed.

We headed southwest, passing by a few mountains and finding shelter in a warm little den after dark. The next morning, we traveled northeast through a forest, crossing lands covered in snow, and we even walked across a frozen river.

We pressed on through the endless night, driving away the nightmares and ghosts.

Finally, a field flashed before us on the other side of the river. It turned out not to be so far away.

The two of us came to a stop there.

As the little mountain goat joyfully pounced about the field, I started to prepare for life in the field ahead.

The Little House

I want to build a house for the little mountain goat that will keep out the wind, rain, and wily foxes.

Building a house requires stone, wood, and straw.

There are rocks all over the field. If I take a few back with me every time I go out, in a few days I should have a few dozen, and those few will slowly turn into a full 100. According to my calculations, building a wall on all four sides requires 320 stones, so the little mountain goat and I searched all over. We came and went until we'd collected enough stones.

There was a field of cattails beside the river. They're as pretty as they are durable, and they're perfect for thatching the ridges of a roof.

But that's right—there aren't any ridges yet.

A single tree can prop up the ridge of the roof. There's an old elm tree on the east side of the field. It says, "I'm old, take me away; if I could become a house, that wouldn't be so bad."

And we absolutely must have a fence. What material could the fence be made out of besides the snow-white trunk of a birch tree? If only I had a birch fence. Other materials aren't worthy of being called a "fence." They could only be made into an enclosure or a barricade. The remaining branches of the birch tree can be used too. They can be made into a door, and the ones we found just so happened to make for a very beautiful one.

The little mountain goat served as the foreman.

She was beside me at every moment, supervising each step of the work. Whenever I completed a step, the goat let out a cheery bleating sound to let me know she approved.

I felt full of enthusiasm when I heard her.

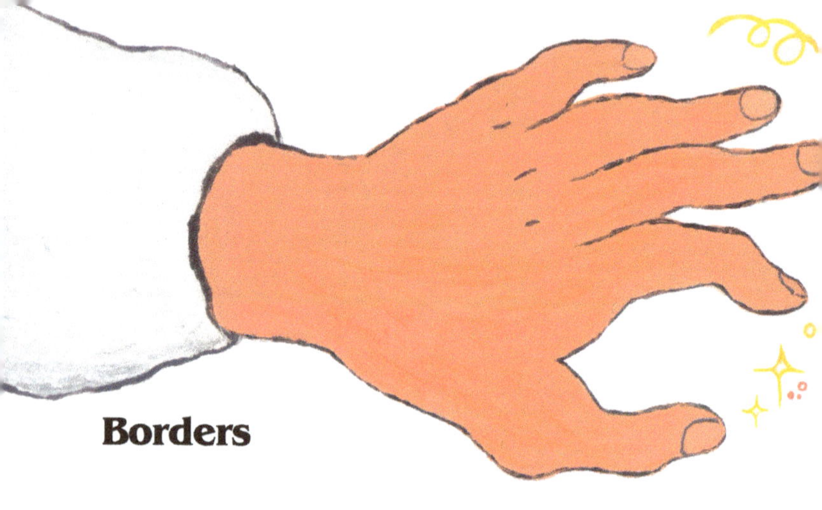

Borders

I opened a map and showed the little mountain goat the border of the field:

To the east is a mountain range, which the map calls the "Changbai Mountain Range." Even farther east is Mount Changbai. There are many villages and forests hidden here. I once went to a village called Thriving Forest. The people there like to draw, so they paint pictures of stories from the past on all of their walls. It was the first time I had ever seen a village covered in drawings.

To the north is a road that runs past a string of places with interesting names. There is the sun, the moon, the seasons, and in between them all is a reservoir called the Milky Way. I spent a sad childhood beside the Milky Way. Little mountain goat, you're completely right. I've come to your side from the heavens to accompany you to this field.

To the south is a river. It flows down from Mount Changbai, meandering to the west until it meets the blue waters of the Bohai

Sea. The river freezes over in the winter. We can walk across the ice, and we can even skate on top of it. Before we do, though, I want to use a rock to polish your hooves. The smoother they are, the faster you'll slide. I'll have no chance of catching you.

To the west is another field filled with rice paddies, but a high-speed rail lies in between. The only way to get there is through the archway below the bridge. If there's time, I'll pick up a few sheaves of rice for you. The sheaves taste just like cooked rice. But mountain goats don't eat rice, so you're probably not familiar with the taste. You'll know what rice is like after a few bites.

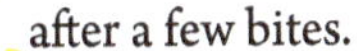

"The border of the field isn't very far away," I assured her. "We can reach it in 16 days."

A Hot Stone

There's a hot stone in the forest to the east. If you just hit it a little it warms up. I was surprised to find that such a stone existed. Don't you think it's weird?

"It's too cold out! My little hooves are frozen stiff!" the little mountain goat bleated.

"Your hooves have always been stiff," I corrected her, "but I understand what you mean. You must be really cold." I tapped the hot rock a little and then handed it over to the goat.

When the little hooves were hot, they left a watermark behind as they plodded across the frozen river.

I shivered as I lay down in the wooden room. The little mountain goat kicked the hot stone over to me, and it landed right in my hands. I opened up the wooden door and hugged the goat. Her whole body was covered in snow, which slowly melted. The water on the floor formed into a map.

The map was covered with all the places I had gone.

Road Sign

A hedgehog got lost and spent a long while wandering through the field. These vast expanses can create problems. They should be managed better. To this end, we should erect some road signs.

The first road sign pointed to Mount Changbai. The wooden sign hung askew, so the little mountain goat used the tips of her horns to straighten it.

The second road sign read, "Rice paddies. Head two miles to the west." The little mountain goat used her front left hoof to fasten this sign in place.

The third sign read, "Tieling City—the end of the universe. Head 30 miles northeast." The little mountain goat looked to the north, where the road extended across the horizon.

The little mountain goat looked at me and pleaded for me to make another road sign that would point to her home.

"You don't need a road sign," I said. "I'll always be near you. If you ever get lost, just bleat out to me."

The little mountain goat bleated at once.

So after our work was done, I took the goat back to her home.

When the Grass is Short

Early in the spring, I spent all my time accompanying the little mountain goat. The scent of grass left her completely restless. She ran all across the field.

Look at that faraway pasture! The little mountain goat ran ahead, but she couldn't find the grass. She looked back again and noticed a spot of grass in front of the door. So the goat ran on back, only to find that there was no grass there at all.

The little mountain goat chased the grass as I chased her. My forehead was soon dripping with sweat, but we kept running across the field, to and fro. Wherever we went the grass was simply too short, though. We couldn't make head or tail of it.

That night, there was a gentle rain and a breeze swept through the field. The next morning, the little mountain goat woke me up with a start.

"Bleat! Bleat! Bleat!"

There was newly sprouted grass all across the field, a lush layer of grass—no doubt about it.

The little mountain goat didn't dare to act without thinking, so she shyly stood inside the fence, afraid that it might slip away once again.

How Heavy is the Little Mountain Goat?

When the little mountain goat was born, she weighed exactly nine jin—no less, no more. An old copper scale never tells lies. One jin is one jin, two liang is just that.

Now the little mountain goat weighs 28 jin. No more, no less—exactly 28. How much grass did the goat eat between when she weighed nine jin and her current weight of 28 jin? How much water did she consume?

Everything that can be eaten in the field belongs to the little mountain goat. She eats as much as her body allows, and she drinks as much as she likes. There's grass in spring and summer,

succulent and sweet; dried grass in the autumn, sweeter than before, and little fruits that serve as after-supper treats; and when she feels hungry in the winter, she need only nuzzle her snout into the snow-covered field, below which there are rations of dried mushrooms and frozen-stiff fruits.

These are the gifts the land has presented to her.

All the nutrients we need come from deep in the ground. The nutrients turn into grass and trees, and they spread across the field. As for the flowers, they're seasoning: they are bitter, sweet, sour, and spicy. When the little mountain goat feels full, she gets her strength, and she gets to taste all the flavors of the field.

The little mountain goat grows up quickly, and she'll soon grow old. The field also grows old, and when its nutrients are gone it turns to sand. I was certainly older than the field then. I told the little mountain goat that I couldn't take care of her forever… My heart fell to pieces, just look if you don't believe—broken-down stones are scattered all across the field.

Revival

When the cocklebur withers, its thorny fruits stick out. The little mountain goat used all four of her legs to drag the fruits back to the field. When temperatures warm up and the snow melts, the thorny fruit forms sprouts as last year's cocklebur comes back to life.

The little mountain goat was terribly excited. She dug out withered grass from the year before. The roots eagerly sprouted new buds, and dandelions revived themselves, as did bristlegrass, and the broadleaf plantains stirred about restlessly. Most of the flowering plants sprouted out from their original roots, the entire chaste tree had revived, and there were the amur roses too. From head to toe, all the bushes and trees were coming back to life.

The little mountain goat hurriedly returned to the fence, where a hawfinch was resting.

It had dropped into the field the previous autumn. It was as withered as the grass. But the land warmed and the snow melted, so the hawfinch had another opportunity to come. The little mountain goat didn't eat or drink—she just spent the whole day waiting for the hawfinch to wake up.

The hawfinch was asleep. It didn't move an inch.

All the many things recover. Can the hawfinch recover too?

The Only Goat

The little mountain goat is the only goat in the field.

Originally, the hares also wanted to stay here. But I recommended a different field to them, and they carried on there just as happy as they'd always been. I even brandished a stone to drive the voles out of the field. Such wretched creatures are not welcome here.

I became increasingly narrow-minded, but I didn't know how to overcome it.

I told the magpie at the top of the tree that the field only belonged to the little mountain goat, and I asked the magpie to tell everyone in the field. With a screech, the magpie flew away and spread this news to every corner of the field. It was very effective. Just as effective as holding a news conference.

Now everything was perfect. Only the little mountain goat was left in the field, along with me. I looked her over carefully every day, and this was enough.

When the little mountain goat grazed, I sat to the north. Someone from Ningbo City was raising bees there. I told the buzzing bees that there were no vitex shrubs here. They were in the shrubbery to the west.

When the little mountain goat slept, I sat in the north. The northern wind was quite strong in those days, so I blocked it for her.

When the little mountain goat stared off into space, I sat around the wild chrysanthemums and whistled. One can't stare into space without music.

The little mountain goat is the only goat under the sun.

Big and Small

Of course we won't refuse kind-hearted visitors and neighbors.

A hunchback entered our field. He told us that a strong wind had blown away his haystack, so his calf had nothing to eat. I took him to a field of alfalfa with enough leaves growing for his calf to eat for three days and three nights.

A pheasant fell into our field. He'd been hunted by a kestrel. The little mountain goat carried the pheasant on his back over to our little house to hide. I brandished a branch to shoo away the kestrel, standing between the two on the side of the pheasant. That's right: between the little mountain goat and everyone else, I stand with the goat.

Beneath the grass live the crickets, earthworms, mole crickets. When she encounters them, the little mountain goat always makes room. They are the original inhabitants of the field. Could they really have come here before the little mountain goat and I did?

The little mountain goat and I stay together. We often go to visit our neighbors, and they come to see us.

Our world is very small. So small that there's only room for us.

But our world is also very big—big enough for everything that is good.

Neighbors

Our neighbors don't come by often.

I gave a few potatoes to the badger by putting them at the entrance to his hole and then leaving. I didn't want to want him to thank me, so I didn't give him the chance to do so. Asking someone to thank you is just making trouble for them, and this would only cancel out the nice feeling I'd created by giving him potatoes.

The crabs in the rice paddy rarely come out. I explained their habits to the little mountain goat, and after we left, we passed through the archways beneath the bridge to return to the field. The crabs live quite far away from us, but I still needed the little mountain goat to understand some things about them so that if she came across the crabs one day, she wouldn't be caught off-guard.

We looked over our neighbors carefully from a distance, offered them some pleasantries when necessary, and then left.

A flock of wild geese quacked away as they dropped in to greet the field below.

The little mountain goat raised her head to bleat out, "Welcome back!"

I lay down beside the little mountain goat and counted. "One, two, three…" The number of geese that left last year was the same number returning this year. They weren't missing a single goose—it was wonderful!

One Day

It's true: all the days in the field are mostly the same. Yesterday, today, tomorrow, and the day after that—they all blur together.

'With the little mountain goat at my side, the days are never tedious. Every day is fresh, every day is like an epic poem.

Early in the morning, the little mountain goat grazes in the south. I sit by her side and watch the clouds. One cloud turned into a little mountain goat, trying to get my attention. I didn't fall for it. At every moment I can hear the sound of the little mountain goat chewing.

At midday, the little mountain goat basks in the sun to the east. I form my fingers into a triangular ruler to measure the length of the mountain range. I calculate how many days it will take us to get to the mountains.

Later in the afternoon, the little mountain goat sings toward the north while I wave about a stick. I don't know how to conduct an orchestra, so the cadence is quite erratic. The grass seeds get shaken out to the ground. Pit-a-pat, pit-a-pat. The katydids are scared silent. Hey! This is the little mountain goat's concert. They should sing at another time, anyway.

The little mountain goat watches the sunset in the west. Another day has passed us by. Another day. One less day the little mountain goat and I can spend together.

Each day I wonder: is there any way to make these beautiful days last longer?

Names

The little mountain goat has many names.

She's called "Little Beast" because when she gets angry, she's ferocious like a little beast and could even knock a tree down. I call her this quite often.

"Little Tomb Egg" is another name. It means the same thing as "Little Rascal," but I call her "Little Tomb Egg." I'm not making this up.

Another name is "Little Horn." Her horns are very radiant. Not even the shrubs can hide them from view. She often rubs her horns against stones to grind them down. But when she does this, she looks more like a baby goat. This tells me she doesn't want to grow up.

I call her "Little Deer" because her eyes are the same as a deer's eyes. By lowering her head, drops of water fall from them. They aren't tears—they're a spring.

I call her "Little Potato," "Little Radish," and "Little Bean Sprout" when she's like a vegetable. Sometimes I call her "Little Steam Bun," "Little Pastry," and "Little Meat Pie" when it fits. "Little Hooves" is another name I like. These names can only be used for a short period of time, maybe a few hours or even a few minutes. And some names I could only use once. For example: "Little Thing."

I wrote these names on a leaf and carved them into stone.

These names fill the field. Wherever you go, you can always see her name.

Wherever the names appear, you can find the little mountain goat.

The little mountain goat is everywhere in the field.

A Sentence for a Leaf

The little mountain goat has one thing to tell you: when the wind blows through the yellow leaves of the big poplar tree beside the river, the sound of innumerable little bronze bells will sound as they fall to the ground.

The two of us set a new rule.

We would only say warm words to each other, which the field could listen to. For every sentence I speak, I'll go and pick up a yellow leaf. Three sentences means three leaves, and ten means ten leaves. If I speak one thousand or ten thousand, then all the yellow leaves of the tree will be yours.

A Gentle Reminder

I want to leave the field for a few days and go to a place where I'll take a test. I said a few parting words to the little mountain goat.

When you ask the sun for the time,
the sun will tell you if it's morning or midday,
midday or afternoon. The sun won't lie to
you. It has never lied to anyone. Sometimes
the sun doesn't stick out its head. This scam
is the work of dark clouds,
but it has nothing to do
with the sun.

There are a few kinds of grass you
can't eat. Grass covered in dew, the ears
of corn, frosted castor bean leaves, and
sweet potato seedlings on the ground.
Don't touch these things no matter
how fresh they taste—they'll hurt your
body. Stick to the alfalfa and milkvetch.
It's an old flavor, but it fits you the best.

Don't be afraid when a mouse enters a house. If you can screech like a cat, then they'll run away, and if you can't do that, then just call me over. I can hear your voice even when I'm outside of the field.

A Few Things to Note When Climbing a Mountain

It's a big event when the little mountain goat wants to climb a mountain. When you climb the mountain, there are even more things to pay attention to than stones on the mountain path.

You need to bring rations with you, and you don't want to pack too light. You're so thin, so you'll need things to eat along the way. That said, you won't want to bring too much, either. You can't carry your luggage if it's too heavy.

Don't walk out front. The snakes in the undergrowth like to tease whoever walks in front. But walking at the back is even worse. Who can say for certain what will happen?

Use your eyes to draw. Give it a try. They can paint any color.

Use your legs to observe. Climbing a mountain is like watching a movie. Each step has a story, and the next step will have another story too.

When you're tired, take a break. Listen to the insects of the autumn. They'll make noise all along this path. Even if you don't understand what they're saying, just listening will calm you down.

Visiting the Forest and the Hillside

The two of us visited the paper birch forest.

The little mountain goat looked at the tallest paper birch tree and counted the golden leaves on it.

One leaf, two leaves, three leaves, four. Five leaves, six leaves, seven, eight, nine… A breeze blew by and the leaves flew through the air. Even when the trunk of the birch is bare, it's still a beautiful sight. It's just that it's not quite as pretty as it was with the leaves.

The little mountain goat couldn't bear to keep counting, so she bowed her head and returned.

"The leaves are all gone. The tree isn't as pretty now," she said.

The two of us left the hillside behind. The field was just ahead.

The little mountain goat mumbled to herself: "There were so many pretty leaves. One leaf, two leaves, three leaves, four. Five leaves, six leaves, seven, eight, nine."

"Look back," I said. "You'll regret it if you don't."

The little mountain goat did as I said, and the sight entranced.

Before her was a hillside covered in a sheet of gold.

The leaves had all fallen, so the trees weren't as pretty, but the hillside was even more beautiful than ever before.

Visiting Other Things

We visited the things near the field. It took us an entire week.

We visited the moonlight. We stood on a dike where we could be closer to the moon.

"The moonlight's lit up the field," said the little mountain goat.

"It also lights up everything outside of the field," I said. "Its benevolence is even greater than the field's."

A little wolf who'd lost his way was rushing along the road. The moonlight lit his path all the way to the mountain ridge in the east.

"Thank you, moonlight!" said the little mountain goat.

We also visited a river that was on the way. The river had a tiresome task. It rushed along day and night, transporting water downstream. The parched plants along the way needed its waters to drink.

The little mountain goat said, "Big river, I've come to see you off."

We also visited a cricket. He was an industrious singer. He sang all through the summer, and when the fall came, he was tired, but he still had to fret about his wintertime performance: he didn't have any new music. He needed the encouragement of an audience.

"I've heard your song," the little mountain goat said. "Although it's just a melody, I think it's very nice."

We visited the sleepless nightingales and the injured fox. The fox's right hind leg had been pierced by a thorn, and she had lost a good deal of blood. We even visited a lonely goose who was perched beside the marsh.

The little mountain goat said, "You're not alone. You have a friend. That friend is me."

Sunsets and Rainbows

There are a few things that the little mountain goat noticed for the first time, such as sunsets and rainbows.

Three days in a row I sat on the fence and watched the sunset with the little mountain goat.

The first day, the shiny white bullet train darted into the red clouds. The little mountain goat was stunned, and she bleated without end. The goat was worried that the sunset would burn the train to a crisp, and she was also worried that the fiery clouds would land on the field and ignite it as well. Fortunately, nothing bad like this happened.

The second day, the little mountain goat was more relaxed. She carefully looked over the sunset. A flock of magpies flew through the crimson clouds without suffering a scratch. The goat let out a long sigh, and her little heart felt a flood of relief.

The third day, the little mountain goat's eyes brimmed with tears of excitement. She had realized something when looking at the brilliant sunset. It glowed red hot, but it didn't burn anything. It got close to things, but it never invaded them.

A rainbow only existed for a single minute, but the little mountain goat was stunned for a full hour. She couldn't accept that the rainbow had gone away, and she finally started to cry.

Beautiful things don't last for long, but the love for these things can be eternal.

I said this to the little mountain goat, and a smile returned to her face.

The Ant King

The little mountain goat loves eating wild strawberries even more than alfalfa and rye.

One day, when the little mountain goat went searching for wild strawberries, a colony of ants blocked her path. The troops of ants looked like a stream of water spread out before her.

The first time the little mountain goat saw the ants, she was stunned. They were so small, but like a society.

"What species are you?" the little mountain goat asked directly. "Your numbers are quite impressive!"

"We are from the family of ants, a species known across the world. You really know little about this world," the ant king announced.

The little mountain goat continued her interrogation: "Where did you come from, and where are you going?" As the master of the field, her questions were all perfectly reasonable.

"We came from the rice paddy to the west. We've only just moved to this field. In the future, we may pass through a furrow and go to the faraway hills."

The hills the ant king mentioned were the piles of dirt I had made a few days before. In the eyes of the ant king, these were massive hills. In fact, many things seem massive to ants.

"Do you mean to say you want to live in this field for some time?"

"At least a month. This place isn't half bad. Why are you asking this?" the ant king was in the middle of organizing his troops and was getting a little impatient.

"It isn't bad at all. When I prance about in the future, I'll need to make sure I tread lightly. My little hooves could easily smush you." The little mountain goat looked at her hooves as she said this.

"You act with a gentle hand," said the ant king, praising her appreciatively.

"I'm looking at my hooves, not my hand," the little mountain goat said sternly. Some words cannot be used at random.

And so the little mountain goat changed her habits. She was cautious when she walked down the path, afraid she'd trample the colony beneath the grass.

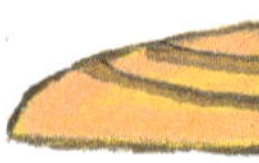

A Mathematical Question

How many little mountain goats are there in the world?

This is a mathematical question, but at the same time it's not.

There are little mountain goats in other places, like Kunming, Ordos, and the outskirts of Ulaanbaatar. And there are even a few in the pastures of New Zealand. But I don't care about them.

I only care about my little mountain goat. I took her to this field, so she represents all the goats in the world.

All the goats are here.

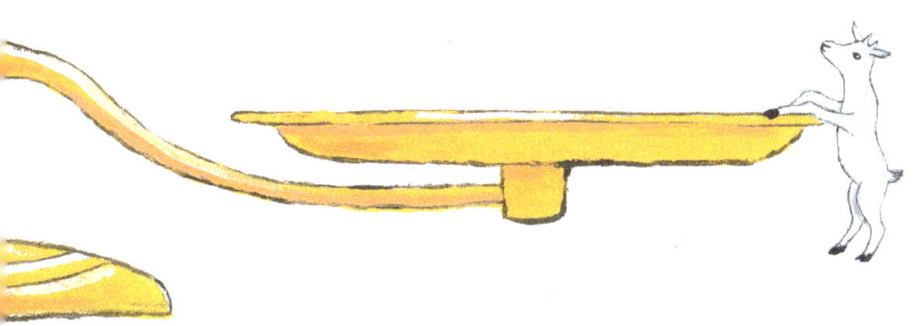

Rays of Light

Every hair on the little mountain goat's body is as white as snow. On days with enough sunlight, she appears to be glowing.

In the morning, the little mountain goat faces westward as she grazes, and her coat glows on the left side of her body. In the afternoon, the little mountain goat faces to the east, and her right side shimmers.

The crow stares at me as if asking, "What are you looking at?"

I nod agreeably.

That night, I have trouble sleeping. The little mountain goat is the most beautiful goat in the world. Everybody thinks this, and I agree.

Therefore, the field my little mountain goat lives in is the most beautiful field, the grass she eats is the best-tasting grass, and the fence behind her is the most stylish fence.

So as for the person beside her? As for me? I fall asleep with a happy heart.

The little mountain goat says, "I'm not the most beautiful goat; I'm just the luckiest…"

Tolerance

Little mountain goat, I'm afraid I'll spoil you.

You flipped over the fence, and I got angry at you. You bleated incessantly outside the fence. But before the clouds rolling in had a chance to fly over our heads, I forgave you.

You treated the poisonous sweet potato sprout like a snack—how stupid? So I yanked the sweet potato away and sternly scolded you. You turned around and left. I heard you bleating in the field. I chased after you and led you back.

In this field, the geese give me energy, the nightingales wake me up, and the crickets lull me to sleep.

In this field, the little mountain goat makes me tolerant of everything.

The Little Mountain Goat's Temper

The little mountain goat has a bad temper.

When it's windy and rainy outside, the whole field shakes. I close the door and keep the little mountain goat inside. The goat says, "No, no, no!" as she bangs her head into the door. When she's like this, her temper is bigger than the little house.

We've heard the rumble of a bulldozer far away. It's said that a new bridge is being built. So I made the little mountain goat behave herself and stay in the field rather than letting her run off to a faraway one. The little mountain goat said, "No, no, no!" and charged toward the horizon. When she's like this, her temper is bigger than the field.

The more I spoil her, the more her temper grows.

The more I love the little mountain goat, the more I spoil her.

Another Mountain Goat

Little mountain goat, of the grasses you eat, which is the sweetest? Alfalfa or millet? I tried some. It didn't taste very good. My cookbook doesn't have any recipes with these ingredients. Of course, my cookbook has too many recipes. This isn't a good thing. I need to cut some things out.

If there were a way for me to turn into another mountain goat, then I'd eat what you eat. Anything you've never eaten, I'd test out for you. I'd leave the tasty grass with rich juices for you, and I'd eat what you don't like.

If I turned into another mountain goat, I'd move into a little house. If two goats pressed up close to each other, it would be very warm. If it's too snug, then I'd stick my head outside, or I could stick my hind legs out. This wouldn't be too much trouble.

The morning greeting would be two goats greeting each other. We'd understand each other, so there'd be no need to guess.

"Mie, mie—good morning! Last night I dreamed of grazing with you," I'd say.

"Mie, mie—that wasn't a dream." The little mountain goat would shake her head as she looked at me.

Everyday Life

Harvesting the grass is essential. This way, we can stockpile food for tomorrow or the day after, or even for the next season. There's nothing more important than harvesting the grass.

Giving a name to every rock is also very important. Little round, spiky head, baldy bright, shiny baldly, ten head, food sender, sender food, big big, small small, big small… These names put my knowledge to the test.

There are no limits to studying, and this holds true in the field. The little mountain goat bleats all day, so I study her bleating. The little mountain goat also rolls around, which she learned from me. In the subject of rolling around, nobody is more qualified than me.

Feeling joy, staring off, walking about, gazing at each other… these are other common subjects.

Dictionary

The little mountain goat's language is simple and reserved. For a time, she taught me a new word every day.

"Mie! Mie! Mie!"
—This means, "I'm hungry."
"Mie-mie, Mie!"
—This means, "Take me out to wander. I'm too bored."
"Mie... Mie... Mie..."
—This means, "I'm really sad."

"Mie…"

—This means, "I'm reminiscing."

"Mie, mie, Mie…"

—This means, "I'm really reminiscing over something."

My language is even simpler than the little mountain goat's.

When I'm silent, I always have the little mountain goat on my mind. When I open my mouth, I speak about the field, the rice paddies, the road, the geese, the river. At these times, what I mean is that I miss the little mountain goat.

I Won't Disappear

When the little mountain goat dozes off, I go beside the river and mow the grass. I want to give her a moment of peace.

I can't hear the birdsong or insects over the sound of the sickle. The most frightening thing is that I can't hear the bleating of the little mountain goat either.

Perhaps she'll call out to me, and I'd never know.

I carry a bundle of grass back with me, only to find that the little mountain goat's eyes are full of terror...

"Mie mie mie—I thought you'd disappeared."

Little mountain goat, I won't disappear. When you can't see me, I'm still doing things for you. All I think about is you. The way you run, the way you turn your head, the way you eat grass, the way your eyes brim with tears of excitement.

This field belongs to you and me.

The Me of Now

Ever since I took the little mountain goat into this field, I've drifted further and further apart from the rascals I used to hang out with.

These two friends came to play a game with me. They said that the pond near the forest was full, so we could hold a diving competition. I earnestly warned them that swimming in the pond is dangerous, and I said I didn't like this game anymore. They left, mumbling away. All of us knew that our former friendship had ended.

There were a few other friends who liked to climb on rooftops and then jump down from them. They'd do it over and over again, sometimes for three days in a row. I warned them about the stupidity of jumping from a roof and said they shouldn't do it again. "It's bad for the house and bad for your legs, so you might as well quit," I told them. They just stared at me blankly as I walked away.

That was how we parted ways.

"Mie! Mie! Mie!"

As soon as I returned to the field, I headed straight for the little mountain goat.

She was hungry. I hurried deep into the forest. The mulberries in my pocket jostled up and down. Yesterday, I'd promised the little mountain goat I'd give her dinner tonight.

I'm not the same person I used to be. Back then, I laughed all day and didn't have a care in the world. Today, I have a field and a little mountain goat. They need me, so I need to be reliable.

A Loud Noise

I left the field and went to a distant place.

I stood below a big tree in the city, and I spoke about survival with the sparrows that filled the tree. When I looked up to the treetop, the image of the little mountain goat poised in the middle of the field flashed through my mind. The little sparrows chirped, telling me their thoughts. But all this noise couldn't hide the call of the little mountain goat.

"Mie! Mie! Mie!"
The little mountain goat was hungry.
I heard this crystal-clear.

Quantities of Food

After the first time the little mountain goat encountered a snake, she went on a diet.

In the past, all of her meals consisted of alfalfa, but now she could only eat a little. She couldn't finish a bundle of grass in an entire day. The little mountain goat believed she could become as thin as a worm. After a few days, the little mountain goat's health began to deteriorate. Even the usual light in her eyes was dimming.

Little mountain goat, forget about that snake. You don't need to have the same body as a snake. Only a snake should look like that. Can't you see that the snake can't stand because it doesn't eat enough, and it can only slither about?

Little mountain goat, you should be happy in the field. That's when you look the best, and this requires strength. You'll also need to help me move a few stones out of the field. But now you couldn't even help me complete half of the task if you tried.

Little mountain goat, you should eat to your heart's content.

Little Hooves

The little mountain goat has four hooves. She couldn't have any more or any less, just like other goats.

The four hooves look like two pairs of black leather shoes.

I took the little mountain goat through the archways beneath the high-speed rail and over to the rice paddies. The little mountain goat was prancing about with joy. She got covered in mud and was soon a complete mess. In the middle of the day, I took her to the river for a bath. She twisted and turned, trying to break free. Without wasting a word, I put her front hooves into the water, and after struggling with her for a while, I gave up. I quickly cleaned her two hind hooves.

Now the four hooves looked just as radiant as they did in the past—two pairs of black leather shoes, a fancy brand.

Idling Away The Time

There are many sunny and cloudless days in the field. At these times, the sun is definitely warm, and it heats up many nooks and crannies. The shade behind the house is cool, but the sunlight gradually lights up this space, making up for whatever heat missed the structure.

On these kinds of days, I idle away my time with the little mountain goat. We spend entire days rolling about in the field. The little mountain goat's muddy body is covered in the golden blades and sheaths of grass. It looks like she's draped in a golden coat.

I'm just like the little mountain goat. I also wear a golden coat.

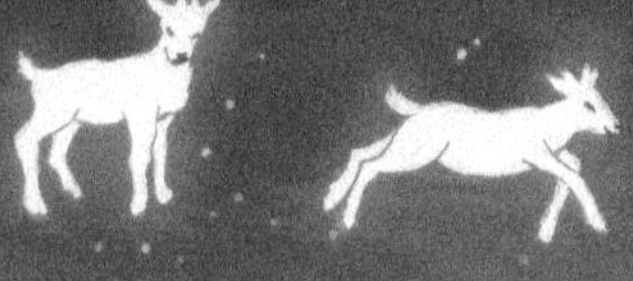

Meaningful

If there wasn't a little mountain goat in the field, then none of the grasses lining it would have any meaning. The sky wouldn't have any meaning either.

The mountain range, river, rice paddies, and highway… none of these would have any meaning.

The birdsong wouldn't be pleasant—it would be static; the crickets wouldn't be singers—just little black bugs; the wind would just be air moving—reckless and boorish but not gentle.

The world is patches of darkness that have been stitched together. The little mountain goat is a lantern that lights the field. She leaves the world with one less patch of darkness.

Birthday

In the first 80,000 hours before the little mountain goat was born, I sat on the coast, lonely as could be. One day, I got on a relative's boat and went fishing just off the coast. The fishing boat sailed along the coastline, gradually entering that world of deeper blue.

Just over my head appeared a snow-white mountain goat, standing above the deep blue. She bowed her head and looked at me as if she wanted to say something.

"If I'm not mistaken… you're a mountain goat," I said first.

The mountain goat nodded to confirm I was correct.

"You want to return to the land and graze with a flock of goats," I continued. "Isn't that right?"

It was a guess, but the goat nodded her head again.

"I… I can't help you… Unless it rains, then you'll come down with the rainwater," I said.

I raised my head and looked up at the clear sky. I was full of despair. And then a gust of wind came along and blew the cloud that looked like the goat away.

Is the little mountain goat that white cloud I saw long ago? If she is, then the little mountain goat should remember that fishing boat floating about in the water, and she should recall that the boy lying on the deck was a younger version of myself. At that time, she still hadn't entered the human realm. I'd arrived before her, and I waited for her a few thousand hours. She certainly fell down to the earth along with the rain.

But what rain did she come from?

The Little Mountain Goat Gets Sick

The little mountain goat is sick. She shouldn't take a single step out of the field, no matter what happens.

The field has a fence that protects her, and she can sleep peacefully in the little house. I cut down the young bristlegrass and scoop fresh water out of the mountain spring. I've only just noticed this water supply. Only I and the Eurasian hoopoe birds know about it.

Beyond the field is a bad place. I've heard that water runs down the street into uncovered manholes that extend into oblivion, the food and running water isn't good to the taste, and even those tall houses look luxurious but are no good for sleeping. They're full of nightmares.

The little mountain goat is sick, so we can't go anywhere else. The only things in the field are the fence, the little house, and me. It's like a hospital. We have a sick ward and a nurse—everything we need.

A Disaster

The floodwaters rushed through the river dike and covered the field. I need to rebuild some things.

The hole in the dike had to be resealed with rocks, and this took me three whole days of work. But some river water still leaked through, and this left me full of worry. I was constantly mending little cracks.

The plantain herbs were completely submerged, so I dug up a canal to send the water away. The canal led to a low-lying area and eventually back into the river.

The little mountain goat stood gloomily on the fence. Her four legs were covered in mud. She seemed to be asking me, "Am I the same little mountain goat as before? Can I go back to being the goat I used to be?"

I took a bucket of clean water and gently cleaned away the dirt. My cheeks were streaming with tears as I cursed the floodwater.

Everything can return to normal. It just needs time. In a few days, your coat will be as white as snow again, and your four little black hooves will shine. The fence and little house will glow again, too, and our days in the field will be just as beautiful as they were before.

Disposition and State of Mind

The disposition of the field is sometimes good and sometimes bad. It can be cloudy or clear, windy or rainy, and it snows too.

This doesn't bother the things in the field. They can always adapt.

When it rains or snows, the plants sway in the wind as their roots silently absorb the moisture. When it's sunny outside, the earth is calm, and the plants make the most of the opportunity. They bloom and bear fruit.

The little mountain goat and I have also been hardened by the weather.

When the little mountain goat is sad, I cheer her up; when I feel gloomy, I look at the warm eyes of the little mountain goat.

We depend on each other in such a way.

Licking

The little mountain goat can lessen one's pain with a lick.

On one occasion, when I was collecting wild roses, the plant's thorns stabbed my arm and hand so deeply that they drew blood. The little mountain goat stood inside the fence and silently inspected my wound.

"It's no more than a scratch. Just give it a few days and it'll be better. If one day isn't enough, then give it three; and if three isn't enough, then give it half a month."

I crushed some duckweed leaves and applied them to the wound. It felt a lot better afterward.

But the little mountain goat still wouldn't come out to eat the fruit.

"Little mountain goat, I hurt myself picking this fruit for you. But I'd willingly do it again."

The little mountain goat stepped outside the fence and licked the wound on my hand. After this, it didn't hurt anymore. Next, she licked my arm, and it also stopped hurting.

This happened last night at nightfall. I wrote it down so I won't forget.

She Can Do Anything

The old man at the hydrological station is no fun. All he talks about is boring stuff.

Here come his questions again:

"I don't understand. What does the little mountain goat have to offer? She can't carry things on her back like a donkey, she can't keep up with a golden retriever and retrieve an ax for you, and she can't cuddle with you like a cat and keep you warm. The little mountain goat is even worse than a rooster—she can't wake you up!"

"Ok, you old geezer," was my official response.

The little mountain goat can't do these things. But what can she do? She lends me her strength and helps me move rocks, she brings me light day and night, and though her singing voice isn't as resounding as that of a rooster or golden retriever, I still can't help but imitate her…

The little mountain goat can do anything.

How Many Seconds in a Day?

The little mountain goat and I passed another day together.

A single day is too short. It's just 24 hours. It's much too little time: just 1,440 minutes. Too short, indeed—a mere 86,400 seconds...

I spent 86,400 seconds with the little mountain goat! So many seconds... and yet it isn't enough. Just think about it. In 86,400 seconds, how many of those can we spend looking at each other's eyes? How many seconds can we spend listening to each other speak? Then consider this: how many seconds will it take to go to the road on the field? How many seconds can we spend talking to neighbors about the weather? How many seconds do we spend tending the grass and grazing? How many seconds are spent repairing the dike?

A single day passes us by in 86,400 seconds. How many of them have I wasted?

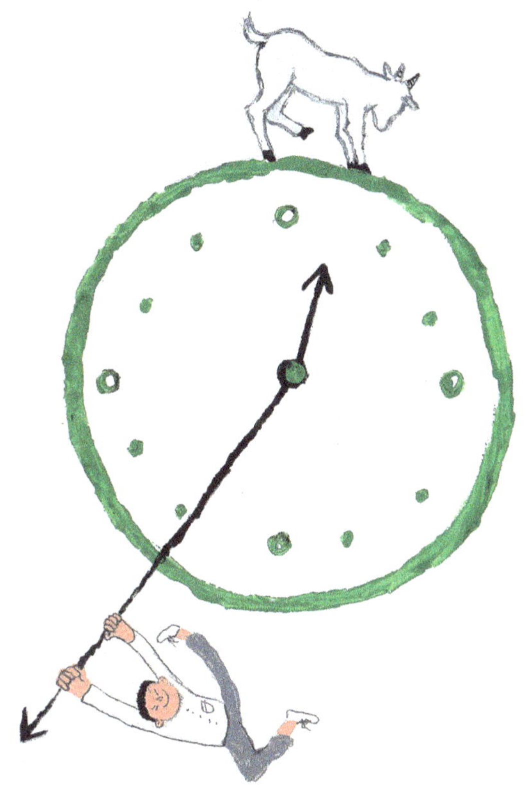

Everyday Routines

Breathe in deeply and appreciate the scent of the field. There are all kinds of plants, and beneath them is the soil— don't let any of them go.

Close your eyes and keep the moonlight with you; put the first rays of sun that stream across the horizon into your sight.

Listen carefully. Hold the songs of birds and insects in your ears, and keep the breathing of the world there too.

We can
take the field away
with us.

Where Have the Birds Gone?

Beginning that first day, the little mountain goat and I started paying attention to the birds flying overhead. This was an important matter.

On the first day, there were 36 birds. Twenty-seven were geese who went south. The goose at the back of the flock was called the lonely goose. He hurriedly headed south. The little mountain goat and I cheered him on, hoping he could catch up with the rest of the flock. The rest of the birds were sparrows, magpies, and redstarts.

On the second day, there were 25 birds. The majority were sparrows and magpies, but there were also ravens. They were headed west to the rice paddies to forage for food. The little mountain goat reminded them that the sage plants in the field were bearing seeds, which would make for a nice main course. A few

sparrows accepted the invitation and dropped down into the field. They walked about pecking at the sage seeds. The little mountain goat was very happy. She stood on the fence and bleated. I was very happy too.

On the third day, there were 18.

On the fourth, 13.

By the fifth, there were only two. The little mountain goat asked me, "Where have all the birds gone?"

On the sixth day, I led her to the eastern forest to look for birds. We could hear chirping far away. It turned out the birds who'd stayed behind were holding a meeting. They needed to discuss how to get through the winter.

The little mountain goat bleated gleefully and entered the forest. She had some ideas that she wanted to share.

Winter

The geese disappeared across the horizon, carrying the autumn away with them. The plants in the field withered, and the cracks between the vegetation grew noticeable.

The little mountain goat couldn't sleep during the day, and she couldn't sleep at night either. She was waiting for news from the far shore of the river to arrive. It was said that a goat over there had been injured, and this bad news caused the chilly air inside the fence to feel that much chillier. It also left the little mountain goat exceptionally anxious.

She urged me to leave the field and go somewhere warm for the winter.

But I won't leave the field. If we hadn't spent a winter here, would spending the summer and fall here be worth it? How could I look forward to the spring?

In the great north, plants that can't make it through the winter are only gorgeous once: they don't understand rebirth and eternity.

Preparing for the Winter

You have to prepare if you want to make it through the winter... The little mountain goat and I spent a long time doing just that.

She was industrious from dusk till dawn preparing goods. She worked so hard that her body grew thin and her face wan. I felt terrible about this.

Sometimes I didn't sleep for an whole night. I was rushing in and out of the field collecting alfalfa and wheat. I also had to prepare goji berry sauce. The little mountain goat needed these things, and I wanted her winter to be a warm one.

"You're too tired. You need to rest," I told her.

"I don't know what rest is."

"If you don't rest, then I won't."

"Fine. Let's nap then."

Sometimes I slept beside the archway beneath the bridge, sometimes I slept beside the rice paddy, and sometimes I slept beside the field. I saw the little mountain goat joyfully prancing about in my dream, the sun shining brightly on the field, the plants full of life.

The spring came again.

Stories From Language Class

Language class is back in session. The little mountain goat is teaching me some more goatspeak.

"Mie-mie-mie, Mie!"

—This means "to plant grass."

"Mie! Mie-mie-mie."

—This means "plucking out the grass."

The little mountain goat wants me to plant more grass so that it covers the entire field. She wants me to pluck out less grass. The field isn't that big. It certainly isn't big enough for us to mess around with it.

"Mie-mie! Mie-mie…" The little mountain goat is saying that pleasant stories are dangerous. When she hears them, she doesn't want to eat or sleep. Depending too much on nice-sounding stories is also dangerous.

As a result, that afternoon I told her a boring story. She fell asleep quickly.

A boring story that makes a little mountain goat sleep is indeed the best story.

Strangers

The little mountain goat spent half a day outside the gate playing. She's grown up, and her body is stronger than it was in the past. The amount of food she eats is much greater too, meaning that I need to prepare even more grass for her. All she cares about is eating grass. She's not upset about a single thing. I'm in charge of mowing the grass. It's tiring but peaceful.

One day, a few people wearing work clothes came to the field. The little mountain goat bleated in their direction. One of the people was fat, and he smiled vaguely as he set up a surveying instrument, which he aimed at the distant dike.

The little mountain goat stared at the surveying instrument. She'd never seen anything like it, and it was indeed a novel sight. But I was afraid that they were invaders and even more would be coming soon.

I'm always on guard against people from elsewhere. I don't know how long our peaceful existence can carry on. I want to build a wall around us, but how can this be done?

I'm also afraid that adults will find out where I've gone sooner or later. They won't allow me to raise a small animal, let alone a little mountain goat.

I cautiously await the arrival of this "doomsday."

The little mountain goat tilts her head and looks at me. She wants to know why I'm unhappy.

The Little Mountain Goat is Gone

The little mountain goat is gone. I realized this after I woke up. I slept for a really long time, from midday to nightfall, and when I woke up I looked out to see what had happened. The first snow had fallen. It was a light, frigid snow, and a chaotic set of footprints extended out across the white blanket.

I have a number of theories.

Maybe goat traffickers abducted the little mountain goat: the little mountain goat's bleating exposed her position and the traffickers found her with ease.

There are no defenses in the field to keep bad people out.

Maybe the little mountain goat got lost. There are too many forks in the road outside. Each fork leads to a city, a forest, or a marsh. Or perhaps there is a road with no end that took the little mountain goat to the horizon.

Perhaps the little mountain goat left without saying goodbye. She decided to return to her marsh from before—to her old way of life.

Then again, maybe the little mountain goat is playing a practical joke. She's hiding in the eastern forest. I hope this is the case.

After three days, I let go of this idea. What practical joke lasts for three days? I looked through the forest. There was no trace of the little mountain goat.

Suddenly, I had a new theory: maybe the little mountain goat has already returned to the field! I rushed out of the forest and sprinted back madly. I nervously opened the fence and went into the little house, only to find that it was empty.

Unfortunately, no miracle had landed in my lap.

Traces

When the little mountain goat was here, you could hear her bleating in the field. After she went away, I could hear her all across the world.

Sometimes I can hear her in the mountains to the east; sometimes her bleating can be heard in the rice paddies to the west.

One day, she was clearly on the other side of the river. I ran all about in a frenzy. I went to the mountain, the rice paddy, and the other side of the river.

The little mountain goat was in none of these places.

I took a high-speed train to the north. Outside the window, I saw the rising and falling of fields, mountains, and forests. There was a flock of mountain goats passing through the forest, running into the distance. I waved at them wildly from the train. My little mountain goat is certainly in that flock.

Or maybe she isn't.

After it snows, she covers the mountains and plains as far as the eye can see, blending into the earth. And after it melts, she becomes clouds and returns to the sky.

November 2020. Written in Shenyang, Fuzhou, Shangrao, Leiyang, Changsha.

Postscript

Over 40 years ago, two brothers were born. The mother had trouble breastfeeding, so the father brought over a mountain goat to serve as the two brothers' "wet nurse." As far as I'm concerned, though, she was a "pet." Several decades later, I can still picture her clearly. The way she expressed joy and ran...

I wrote my first "biography of a pet" in a single go.

I wrote in Shenyang, Wuyuan, Leiyang, and Changshe. I wrote in a wooden house beside a muddy river, on a hotel sofa in Fuzhou, and in a courtyard in Meiling.

I wrote one character at a time, one sentence at a time, one paragraph at a time.

I wrote with tears, sweat, and blood.

I wrote in the early morning, the middle of the day, the afternoon, late at night, and in the wee hours.

I wrote and wrote as the moon fell and the sun came out again.

I wrote and wrote as the autumn ended and it began to snow.

The earth is washed white, the many living things are reborn, and the little mountain goat has returned.

November 25, 2020. In the wee hours.
Written in a little wooden room.